Dot.

Goes Fishing

Dot
Goes Fishing

CANDLEWICK
ENTERTAINMENT

JimHenson
THE JIM HENSON COMPANY

First edition 2020

Library of Congress Catalog Card Number pending
ISBN 978-1-5362-1333-1

20 21 22 23 24 25 CCP 10 9 8 7 6 5 4 3 2 1

Printed in Shenzhen, Guangdong, China

This book was typeset in Brandon Grotesque Bold.
The illustrations were created digitally.

Candlewick Entertainment
an imprint of
Candlewick Press
99 Dover Street
Somerville, Massachusetts 02144

visit us at www.candlewick.com

Contents

. . . .

Chapter 1

· · · · · · · ·

Dot and Dad were in the kitchen. They were making sandwiches—lots of sandwiches. And Dad took making sandwiches, which he called sammies, very seriously. Dad continued assembling.

"Lettuce," said Dad.

"Lettuce!" said Dot.

"Then Dijon mustard,"
said Dad.

"Dee . . . um,
mustard!" said Dot.

2

"And now the best part," said Dad. "Organic maple-smoked salami. Perfect!"

Dad laid the slices of salami on the bread with great care.

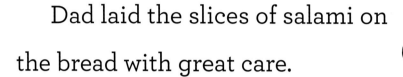

There was a
knock at the door.
It was Dot's friend
Hal.

"Hi, Hal!" said
Dot.

"Hi, Hal," said Dad. "What's
shaking?"

"Hi, Dot! Hi, Mr. C. I just came
by to bring you this." Hal held out
his hand. In it was a rock.

"It's a rock," said Dad.

"Your lucky rock!" said Dot.

"Yup," said Hal. "I thought you could use it on your first-ever fishing trip."

Hal gave Dot the rock.

Dad looked at Hal. He looked at the rock.

"Here's something else that rocks!" he said. "My super-duper fishing-trip sammies."

Dad gave Hal an organic maple-smoked salami sammy.

Chapter 2

· · · · · · · · ·

Dad went out to put the fishing gear in the car.

"Your dad seems really excited," said Hal.

"He is," said Dot. "And he'll be even more excited when he sees this!"

Dot held out a large plastic frog.

Scratch looked at the frog and barked.

"A frog?" asked Hal.

"It may look like a frog," said Dot, "but it's actually a Fisherman Joe Fish-Finder."

"A Fisherman Who What-Finder?" asked Hal.

"I'll show you," said Dot. "It came with a video. See, my dad goes fishing all the time, but he never comes home with any fish. Not once, ever. So Mom and I got this to help him. Watch!"

Dot opened the app on her tablet.

Fisherman Joe appeared on the screen. "Using the fish-finder is as easy as one, two, three—fish! Just attach the fish-finder to a line and place it in the water. It uses sonar technology to scan the area and

detect fish. All you have to do is watch on your tablet or smartphone."

Fisherman Joe reached overboard and pulled in a huge fish.

"Wow!" said Dot and Hal together. That was real fishing! Dot knew it was exactly what Dad needed.

Chapter 3

· · · · · · · · ·

Dot and Dad were in their boat. They cast their lines. Then Dad leaned back.

"Ahh," he said, "nothing left to do now but relax and enjoy each other's company—and the beautiful view!"

"Or we could skip all that stuff and catch some fish," said Dot. She pulled out the Fisherman Joe Fish-Finder.

"What is that?" asked Dad.

"It's a fish-finder!" said Dot. "Surprise!"

"Well, I usually like to catch fish on my own," said Dad, "you know, just using my wits."

"But Dad, the fish keep winning!"

"Ouch!" said Dad. "And that's not

exactly true, but I'm happy to give it a try."

Dot was excited. She tied one end of the fish-finder to the boat and put the other end in the water.

"Look, Dad!" she said. "Fish! All over the place!"

"Okay!" said Dad. "Now we can get back to relaxing while we wait for those little guys to get hungry."

Dot frowned. "Wait?" she asked.

"Yup, and speaking of being
hungry, who wants one of my super-
duper sammies?"

Dot nibbled on her sandwich, but

she couldn't concentrate on her food. She kept looking over the side of the boat. There were plenty of fish in the water, but none of them were biting.

Chapter 4

· · · · · · · · ·

"**W**hat's taking so long?" asked Dot.

Dad leaned back into his resting pose. "They'll bite when they're ready," he said.

"Did you remember to bait the hooks?"

"Yup, with Grade A juicy worms," said Dad.

"Blech," said Dot. "Maybe the fish don't like worms."

"Trust me," said Dad. "Fish love worms."

Dot tore off a tiny piece of sandwich and tossed in into the water. *SNAP!* The fish ate it right up. "Dad, the fish like your sammy."

"They ought to," said Dad. "That's some primo salami!"

Dot tossed more pieces of

sandwich into the water. And more,

and more. Soon there were fish

everywhere!

Dot showed Dad her tablet.
But then, one by one, the fish
disappeared. Something was
swimming up from the deep. . . .

Chapter 5

It was a fish, and it was HUGE.

Then Dot's tablet screen turned black. Everyone was quiet.

"Um, Dot?" said Dad. "I think that fish might have taken . . ."

The line went taut.

"It ate the fish-finder!" yelled Dot.

The boat started to move — fast.

The fish was swimming away, taking

Dot and Dad with it!

"Don't worry, Dot," yelled Dad.

"I've got you!"

WHOOSH!

"Where is he taking us?" yelled Dot.

The boat sailed across the water,

then turned and zipped back.

They went across the lake and
back around again. Dot saw a large
rock sticking out of the water. They
were heading right for it!

SNAP!

"The fish-finder! It's gone!" said Dot.

"Oh, no, it's not. We're not done yet," said Dad. "That fish-finder has a GPS tracker in it, right, Dot?"

"Yup," said Dot.
"So we can
look on your
tablet and see
where it's headed."

"Good idea, Dad." Dot checked
her screen. "It went that way!"

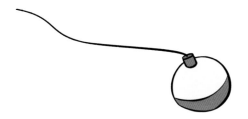

Chapter 6

· · · · · · · · ·

Dad started rowing. The frog moved across Dot's screen.

"Left, Dad! No, right, right! Faster, Dad!"

"That is one fast fish," said Dad. He rowed as fast as he could.

Finally, the fish slowed down. Dad steered the boat into a small bay. "We've got him cornered!" said Dot.

Dad licked his finger and held it up, checking the wind. "Okay! Now it's time for some serious fishing!"

He cast his line, then sat back.

"What do we do now?" asked Dot.

Dad whispered, "We wait."

Dot and Dad looked out at the bobber on the water. It was still.

Dot waited. Then she waited some more.

"Why is it taking so long?" she asked.

"Patience, Dot," said Dad. "Good things come to those who wait."

They waited.

Then the bobber wiggled. It wiggled again. Then it went under!

"Dad!" yelled Dot.

Dad held on to his fishing rod and started reeling.

"Nobody steals my daughter's frog!" he said.

"Go, Dad, go!" shouted Dot.

Dad pulled the line harder and
harder. Dot pulled on Dad.

Together they lifted the pole,
and a huge fish came up out of the
water.

Chapter 7

· · · · · · · · ·

The fish landed in the boat with a *thump!* Something fell out of its mouth and onto the floor of the boat.

Dot and Dad stared at the fish. "I haven't seen very many fish," said Dot, "but I think this is a big one!"

"I'd say so, yes," said Dad. "And look!" He held up the fish-finder. "I think this belongs to us!"

Dad gently lifted the fish.

"What are you doing, Dad?" asked Dot.

He put the fish back in the water.

"So long, big guy!" he said. The fish swam away.

"You're letting it go?" asked Dot.

"Of course," said Dad. "I always let them go."

Chapter 8

· · · · · · · · ·

"Oh," said Dot. "So that's why you always come home empty-handed. Why do you do that?"

Dad looked at Dot. "It's all about catching the fish," he said, "not bringing them home. Fishing is great even when you don't catch anything."

"It is?" asked Dot.

"Sure!" said Dad. "For me, fishing is all about being out on the water, eating tasty sammies, and spending time with someone I love. What could be better?"

Dot looked away. "So I guess bringing the fish-finder and making you chase that ginormous fish all over the lake kinda ruined our time together?"

"No way!" said Dad. "This

afternoon has been the best time

with my favorite Dot-Bot."

Dad gave Dot a big hug.

"It was fun for me, too, Dad," said Dot. "But I'm hungry. Got any more of those sammies?"

"Of course! A fisherman always has to be prepared!"

Dad reached into the cooler and took out a sammy for Dot and one for himself.

Dot and Dad put their feet up and quietly ate.

"Dad," asked Dot, "do you think we'll ever see that big fish again?"

"You never know, Dot," he said. "You never know. . . ."

"So, it turns out that fishing is super fun. The best part is hanging with my dad.

"We're going to go fishing again next week. This time, we'll be ready for that ginormous fish monster. . . .

"And we're going to bring along plenty of sammies!

"Time for me to unplug. This is Dot, signing off for now!"